American edition published in 2020
by New Frontier Publishing USA,
an imprint of New Frontier Publishing Europe Ltd
www.newfrontierpublishing.us

First published in the UK in 2020
by New Frontier Publishing Europe Ltd
Uncommon, 126 New King's Road, London, SW6 4LZ
www.newfrontierpublishing.co.uk

ISBN: 978-1-912858-83-5

Distributed in the United States and Canada by Lerner Publishing Group Inc.
241 First Avenue North, Minneapolis, MN 55401 USA
www.lernerbooks.com

Library of Congress Cataloging-in-Publication Data is available.

Designed by Verity Clark

Printed in China
1 3 5 7 9 10 8 6 4 2

Bear
was
THERE

For Dad.
– S A G

A big thanks to everyone in the
Collaborate Agency for their
input and hard work.

Thank you also to all the team at New Frontier Publishing.
A special thanks to Stephanie Stahl, an
extremely insightful and thoughtful editor,
and to Verity Clark for all her amazing design
talent and expertise.

Sally Anne Garland

Sally Anne Garland

NEW FRONTIER PUBLISHING

LOVE.

The first thing Mouse felt was love,
as he lay in the warmth of his mother's
fur inside a cozy nook of a tree.

As he grew, Mouse felt curious
about the world outside.

"Be careful," his mother whispered.
"There is DANGER. Bear is out there."

Mouse was a little nervous,
but he timidly crept out.

Outside, he smelled the fresh air and gazed in wonder at the world around him. A light breeze was running through his whiskers. Mouse felt **excited**.

But, in the distance, there was a **big dark** shadow.

"Quick!" his mother warned. "It must be Bear." So they scampered away.

Eventually, Mouse ventured into the long green grass of a big meadow.

Flowers and insects danced in the sun's warmth.

He ran across the field; his heart was beating fast.

Mouse felt **happy**.

Mouse came to a clear stream. For the first time, he saw water, and beautiful, shiny fish swimming about.

Mouse felt **amazed**,

but in the distance his mother called to him:
“Careful, Little Mouse. Bear could be close.”

So he did not stay.

Soon Mouse grew bigger and bigger, and it was time for him to leave his mother's home to build his very own.

He journeyed farther into the woods and settled in a safe, towering tree. He happily scampered and scurried around until one day . . .

Mouse was playing in the soft grass when he heard the dry snap of a branch behind him.

Someone was there.

Mouse darted behind some leaves.

A **huge**, familiar shadow, a lot bigger and a lot scarier than before, was looming over him.

It was **Bear.**

Trembling, Mouse looked up as Bear gazed down. The woods were silent. Mouse was surprised at how kind Bear's eyes seemed.

Then, with a sniff and a soft rustle of leaves, Bear gently padded away.

Maybe Bear isn't so scary after all, thought Mouse.

Time passed.

Mouse watched the wind play with the fallen brown leaves. His neighbors moved away and Mouse felt alone. The air became frosty and quiet.

Mouse shivered as the ground
grew cold and hard beneath him.

Then winter came.

Mouse was woken up by an icy wind. It was roaring through the trees. Branches crashed and the woods were dangerous.

Mouse felt **afraid.**

He scrambled away, straight into the raging storm.

Mouse struggled through the snow, shivering and lost. Suddenly, Bear was THERE, but Mouse did not feel scared. Instead, he felt a strange relief, for he knew Bear was surely heading toward a shelter.

Mouse began to follow him.

Through the frosty gales and biting cold, Little Mouse kept walking. Ahead, Bear's shadowy bulk lumbered on.

Then Bear disappeared into the opening of a cave.

Using all the strength he had left,
Mouse followed.

As he stumbled inside, he found
Bear curled up, almost asleep, on
the cave's dry floor.

Mouse felt terribly weak, but managed
to climb up to Bear's chin.

Nestling into the warmth of Bear's thick fur, he was no longer alone or afraid.

Mouse felt safe and peaceful.

Bear gently placed his paw on Mouse's little head.

Bear was there, and Mouse felt . . .

LOVED.